SANDRA CLAUS

SANDRA CLAUS

A Tiny Gift to Santa Brings a New Tradition to Christmas

Douglas Clark Hollmann

Illustrations by Frederick James Smith

Merry Christmas
Brianna

Doug Hollmann
Christmas 2003

EUMAEUS PRESS

Annapolis, Maryland

For Megan and Catherine,

who, when they were little,

wanted to do big things,

just like Sandra,

and for their mom, Jan,

who always wanted this story

to be told.

SANDRA CLAUS

Chapter I

Twas the night before Christmas and all through Santa's house, not a creature was stirring, not even a . . .

Well, actually, a mouse *was* stirring. A plump, gentle one named Rudy, to be exact. He was wide awake, sitting on the front steps to Santa's house, his furry little head in his paw.

Rudy sighed and looked up at the night sky. Another Christmas Eve had come and gone. Santa's sleigh was unhitched and parked in its stall, and the reindeer had been bedded down in the barn. The elves were dropping off to sleep, their blankets tucked up under their white-bearded chins. The mice who lived under Santa's house curled up in their nests as Santa and Mrs. Claus blew out the last candle and settled back into their deep feather bed. Santa and his helpers were all worn out from making gifts and delivering them the world over.

Why, then, Rudy wondered, wasn't he sleepy too? Alone now in the quiet, he couldn't say what was bothering him. He loved Christmas as much as everyone else did. He always found bits of wood to whittle into tiny toys for his young ones, and pieces of cheese and bread to gather for their holiday meals. It was the time of year that he relined his family's tunnels with the fragrant cedar shavings left over from the jewelry boxes the elves carved. What a wonderful time his family had each Christmas season!

Why was he restless, Rudy wondered and sighed again, shifting his head from one paw to the other.

Just when he'd given up all hope of an answer, a bright light appeared near the North Star. Rudy saw it out of the corner of his eye and looked up. To his amazement, it seemed to be coming down toward Santa's house! As the light came closer, Rudy could see a shower of tiny ice crystals in the cold night air. Quickly, he jumped off the steps and ducked under them, but he couldn't stop himself from peeking out to see what it was. Looking up through the silver sprinkles that fell around him, Rudy could finally make out a tiny angel, and she was holding tightly onto a tiny wicker basket.

The angel landed on the step in front of Santa's door. She set the basket down and reached in to straighten something. That done, she turned and began to float back up into the air. Rudy watched until the point of light became faint, then he scampered up the steps and looked into the basket. Inside was a beautiful baby girl, no bigger than his own baby mice. The little baby smiled up at him. Rudy was so enchanted that he didn't notice the little angel floating back down behind him.

"And just what are you doing here?" the angel asked in a sweet, yet demanding voice. She hovered just above Rudy, her wings fluttering like a hundred butterflies. "You were supposed to be asleep, like all the rest."

Rudy didn't know what to say; he'd never seen an angel before. He stood there, speechless.

"Well?" the angel asked again. She folded her little arms across her chest and tried to sound stern, but Rudy could see a faint smile on her lips.

"I, I couldn't sleep," Rudy stammered. "I've never seen an angel," he added, "or a tiny baby girl in a basket," he went on hurriedly. He looked down into the basket. "Who is she for?" he asked, suddenly full of questions. "Are you going to leave her here?"

"She's my present to Santa and Mrs. Claus," the angel replied, moving to her left a bit to look into the basket. The angel's face was beaming. "Santa and his wife bring so much joy to children everywhere, but they've never had a child of their own. I thought the nicest gift I could bring them would be a little girl they could raise as their own daughter."

What a terrific idea, Rudy thought, as he looked again at the baby. "But she's so very small," he observed.

"Yes, I know," the little angel agreed. "I've never done this before. I didn't really wish for one so small, but," she shrugged, "that's what I got. Anyway, I'm sure it will be all right. Everything always is where I come from." She fluttered her wings and turned toward Rudy. "You never answered my question," she reminded him. "You were supposed to be asleep, like everyone else, remember?"

"I wanted to sleep," Rudy began awkwardly, "but I just couldn't. Something kept me up."

"Hmm," the little angel said, and what looked like a frown passed across her face (except that, as everyone knows, angels never frown). Then her face brightened. "Maybe you were *supposed* to be here."

"Me?" Rudy asked, bringing a paw up to his chest.

"Yes," the little angel replied. "Maybe you're supposed to watch over this little girl, to make sure she's okay."

Rudy gulped. "I'm only a mouse," he began, but the little angel interrupted him.

"And I'm only a tiny angel," she said, tilting her chin into the air, "yet look what I can do."

Rudy wanted to point out that there was a very great difference between being an angel — even a tiny angel — and being a mouse, but he thought better of it.

"And now, Rudy," the angel said, "you must promise me that you'll never tell anyone about this. The little girl must never know that she was a secret gift delivered to Santa's doorstep early Christmas morning. Promise?"

Rudy nodded vigorously. "I promise," he pledged. He wanted to ask the angel how she knew his name. He didn't remember telling her. He decided angels knew many things he didn't know, and he just better listen and stop asking questions.

The little angel seemed satisfied. "Now," she warned Rudy gently, "you'd better hide. Santa and Mrs. Claus are coming. I can hear their footsteps. I don't want them to see you standing here when they open the door and look out."

Rudy turned and slipped over the edge of the steps while the little angel floated back up toward the North Star. Just as she disappeared from view, the front door opened. Santa stepped out, rubbing his eyes and muttering something about who could be knocking on his door at this hour. He looked down and saw the basket lying in front of him.

"Hello," he cried out loud, "what have we here?" He poked a fat finger inside the basket and suddenly saw the baby. "A baby?" he asked, disbelief spreading across his whiskered face.

He picked up the basket. Inside was a note.

"Dear Santa," he read aloud, "here is a Christmas present you've always wanted." He turned the note over, but nothing else was written on it. He looked up. "Who could possibly have sent this?" he asked, but his question went unanswered.

Rudy wanted to rush out from under the steps and tell Santa all about the angel, but he remembered his promise in the knick of time. He stayed hidden just beyond the light streaming through the opened front door.

Santa looked back into the basket. "Mrs. Claus," he called excitedly over his shoulder. "Mrs. Claus, come here. I've got something wonderful to show you!"

Mrs. Claus appeared in the doorway, wrapping her purple robe around her. "Santa, what are you doing out here in the night air? Come inside before you catch cold."

"Look what I found!" he replied, holding the basket out to Mrs. Claus. "It's a baby girl. *Our* baby girl," he explained, waving the note. "It says so, right here," he said, handing Mrs. Claus the small slip of paper.

Mrs. Claus quickly read the note. She gingerly took the basket from Santa Claus and looked inside. "Oh, she's *beautiful*," Mrs. Claus cried. Santa stood next to her, beaming. "But where did she come from?" Mrs. Claus asked, looking around.

"I don't know," Santa replied. "I came outside and found the basket sitting on the top step."

They both looked back into the basket.

"What shall we call her?" Santa asked, looking up at Mrs. Claus.

Mrs. Claus thought for a moment. "Sandra," she declared. "We'll call her Sandra Claus."

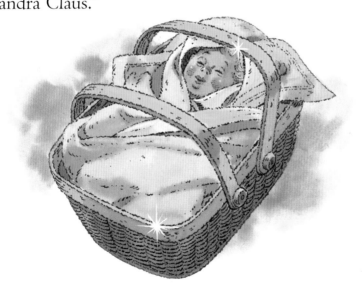

Santa nodded approvingly. "Sandra," he repeated to himself. He liked the name.

"Well, let's get inside," Mrs. Claus said, suddenly all business, "before the three of us catch a chill."

She picked up the basket. Santa put his arm around Mrs. Claus and the two of them went back into the house, carrying Sandra, their baby girl.

Rudy watched them close the front door, leaving him alone again in the dark. Or was he? He looked up at the North Star, but the little angel was nowhere to be seen. He waited a moment longer in case she reappeared, but everything was still. What did it mean, he wondered to himself? Why had he been allowed to stay up and watch the little angel deliver her present to Santa Claus? Why was he chosen to be the baby's guardian?

All of a sudden, Rudy felt very tired. "I'll think more about this in the morning," he thought to himself. Yawning, he disappeared into his mouse hole. In just a few minutes, he too was fast asleep with his little family, far beneath the house where Sandra and her new parents slept so contentedly.

Chapter 2

The months and years passed and Sandra grew up, but she never got very big. In fact, she stopped growing when she got about as high as the top of Santa's slippers. She liked to climb into one and pretend it was a magic sleigh. "Look at me," she would cry out, leaning this way and that as she pretended to zoom around the great kitchen, mimicking Santa's sleigh full of presents on Christmas Eve. Or, she would run out the front door and slide down into Rudy's burrow beneath the front steps to play with his children — Squeak, Nibble, and Nonstop. She and Nonstop would spend hours chasing each other, squealing with delight as they played endless games of Catch-Me-If-You-Can.

Everyone at the North Pole came to love this bright, energetic little girl who was always so willing to help. Sandra loved each one in return, but it was Rudy who became her closest friend. The two of them were the only night owls at the North Pole. Sandra and

Rudy would sit outside at night, stargazing and talking. Sandra was full of questions. One night she asked Rudy how he got his name. Surely, Rudy must be short for something else.

"It is," he said. "Rudy stands for Rudolfo Gonzales Alhambra Smith."

"What!" Sandra exclaimed. Rudy slowly repeated his full name, ignoring the amusement he heard in her voice.

"What kind of name is that?" she asked.

"It's Spanish," Rudy answered.

"Spanish!" Sandra cried. She had been studying all about Europe, and was amazed to find someone at the North Pole connected with such a faraway place. "You came from Spain?" she asked Rudy, her eyes opened wide.

"No, no, no," Rudy said quickly. "My great-great-grandfather on my mother's side was a seafaring mouse who left home in Cadiz, Spain, on board the ship of a famous explorer named Juan Caboto. Juan wanted to find the Northwest Passage to India."

"And did he?" Sandra asked.

"If he had," Rudy said, "I wouldn't be living here. I'd be Rudolfo Gonzales, a fat little mouse living under Juan Caboto's house in Cadiz, for Juan would have been a rich man. Unfortunately, his ship was crushed by ice. My great-great-grandfather escaped here."

"What an adventure," said Sandra. "But what about the name Smith? Where did that come from?"

Rudy shrugged. "There was only one mouse who was Spanish. All the rest were English."

Sandra thought about this for a moment. "So now you're Santa's mouse," she announced brightly.

Rudy smiled. "Yes, I guess you could say that. Besides, I've been to Spain." Sandra looked surprised. Rudy continued. "One time, when I was young, I hitched a ride on Santa's sleigh. Spain was a very dry, warm place, even at Christmastime. No snow. I don't think I would have been happy there."

Sandra nodded her head in agreement. Neither spoke for a while. Then Sandra sighed. "At least you know where you came from," she said quietly. "I wish I did."

Rudy remained silent. Brightening, Sandra turned to look at him. "Rudy, I've never thought to ask you before, but do you know where I came from?"

Rudy didn't know what to do. He coughed behind his paw to avoid having to answer her. He wasn't good at fibbing. "Why, you're Santa's darling little girl," he finally replied.

"No, I'm not," she whispered. "I overheard Santa and Mrs. Claus talking about me one night. I'd slipped downstairs to get a glass of milk and they were in the kitchen. I heard them say they'd found me somewhere. Do you know where I came from?" she repeated, looking at him again.

Rudy had to muster all his strength to keep from blurting out that he knew very well where she had come from, but he remembered the promise he'd made to the little angel. He couldn't break that promise, no matter how much he loved Sandra.

"No, Sandra," he lied, the word cutting through him like a knife. "No, I don't."

She looked away as tears formed in the corners of her eyes.

Rudy put a paw on her shoulder. "Does it matter?" he asked. "You have wonderful parents. You live at the North Pole. And you have me for a friend. Do you need anything more?"

Sandra looked at him and smiled. She wiped away the tears. "You're right," she said, picking her head up. "What else could I possibly want?"

Rudy hugged her. She was so brave. He wanted to tell her the truth, but how would she feel if she found out she'd been delivered in a basket to the North Pole by an angel? She might not even believe him. No, it was right not to tell her. Instead, he just held her in his arms.

Chapter 3

Sandra grew older but no bigger. She hadn't noticed how small she was at first, but gradually she realized she was different. And she didn't like it.

"I was helping Mother in the kitchen today when a chocolate chip cookie fell on me," she said to Rudy one night while they were sitting out on the front steps after everyone else had gone to bed. Rudy couldn't help smiling at the thought of Sandra being squashed by a cookie. Sandra saw the smile on his face and got mad.

"See?" she exclaimed, moving away from him. "Even you laugh at me." She folded her arms and scowled.

Rudy forced himself to look serious, but Mrs. Claus did make huge chocolate chip cookies. "The same thing happened to me once," he told her. "I went into the kitchen one night after everyone was asleep and tried to steal one of those great big cookies. It came tumbling down on me, and I had a hard time getting out from

underneath it!" Rudy didn't mention that he'd eaten his way out, and what a delicious escape it had been.

"Yes, I know you're small too," Sandra agreed, still angry, "but you're a mouse. You *should* be small. I'm a little girl. I should be bigger. I want to be bigger. I want to do big things!"

Sandra's face showed that determined look Rudy had seen a few times before. He tried to think of something she could do. "Why don't you go with Santa this year and help him deliver the toys?"

Sandra considered this for a while. "Hmm. That's not exactly what I want. I mean, I won't actually get to drive the sleigh. Still, it would be fun." She jumped up and went straight to Santa to see what he thought about Rudy's idea. Santa resisted her at first, but finally, after listening to Sandra's pleas, he said yes. Sandra was so excited, she ran to tell Rudy.

"Rudy!" she called out as she slid down into his tunnel, "Santa said I can go with him this year! Isn't that wonderful?"

Rudy was chewing on a biscuit he had found in the kitchen upstairs. He didn't like it; it was dry and tough. "That's great," he mumbled, pulling the pieces of biscuit from between his teeth. "Can I come too?" he heard himself asking. This surprised him, because he hadn't thought about going with Santa in years.

"Of course you can," Sandra declared. "Santa's bound to agree, especially since you've gone with him before. You'll be my guardian angel on the trip!"

Rudy was taken aback. Her guardian angel? He'd never thought about being Sandra's guardian angel, but then he recalled what the little angel had said to him: "Maybe you're supposed to watch over

this little girl." The biscuit, now forgotten, dropped from his little paw. He started to protest, but Sandra had already run off, happier than Rudy had seen her in years.

When Christmas Eve came, Santa climbed into the front seat of the sleigh and grabbed the reins. Sandra and Rudy climbed up behind him and tucked themselves in under a red-and-white-striped blanket that Mrs. Claus had knitted especially for them. They sat high atop the canvas cover that had been folded down over the back of the sleigh. In front of them lay all the Christmas gifts, wrapped in bright-colored paper that glittered silver, gold, green, and red in the moonlight.

"On Comet, on Cupid," Santa cried out, and with a rush the huge sleigh, filled to overflowing with toys, slid off the ground and into the night sky.

"Good-bye," called Mrs. Claus after them. The elves waved and cheered as the sleigh swirled over the barn, whisking snow off the roof as it cleared the peak and headed south. "We'll be back before you know it," they heard Santa call out as he and the sleigh disappeared.

Chapter 4

Santa was very busy that night. He had more houses to visit than ever before. "The number just seems to grow more and more each year," he said over his shoulder. Sandra and Rudy marveled at the farms and rivers they flew over. The sky was filled with diamond necklaces made of stars, and not a cloud was in sight. Sandra and Rudy could see forever as the world below them slept, the children dreaming of sugarplums and fairies.

When they came to a house, Santa would swoop down onto the roof and, in the twinkling of an eye, slip down the chimney with a bag of toys to leave in front of the fireplace. Then he would reappear and climb back into the sleigh once more, ordering the reindeer on to the next house.

The night wore on, and the two friends waited patiently as Santa visited each and every house. Rudy and Sandra hadn't seen another creature since they'd left the North Pole, which was why, while waiting on the roof of a farmhouse in Minnesota, they never heard the cat sneaking up behind them. Rudy was pointing out to Sandra the different colors of the stars.

"You see, they're not all white," he was saying. "That one over there is a brilliant blue. Its name is Sirius, the brightest star in the sky. The one to the left is pale yellow. And the reddish one right overhead isn't a star at all. It's a planet."

Sandra was leaning back to look at the stars Rudy had described, when the cat flashed a paw over the back of the sleigh and snatched her! In one silent movement, Sandra was gone.

Turning to see if Sandra was impressed with his knowledge of astronomy, Rudy saw her vanishing over the edge of the sleigh behind him. He couldn't believe his eyes! He jumped onto the top of the sleigh and saw the cat slinking across the farmhouse roof. Sandra was dangling from his mouth like a rumpled bird that had been plucked from its mother's nest.

"Sandra!" Rudy screamed.

Sandra didn't make a sound. The cat — thick-necked and muscular, its coat a dingy yellow — paused momentarily to look up at Rudy, who shrank from those malevolent eyes. The cat seemed to be considering whether he should go back up and get the mouse standing on the edge of the sleigh, but his mouth was already full. One dinner was enough for one night. He turned and padded off toward the edge of the farmhouse roof.

"Sandra!" Rudy screamed again. Now, being a mouse, Rudy was by nature deathly afraid of cats, except the fat, lazy one named Wreath who liked to curl up under the Christmas tree in Santa's living room. But this was no fat, lazy cat. This was a strong, battle-scarred farm cat, and Sandra was doomed if Rudy couldn't think of something fast.

Oh, where was Santa? Why didn't he come back up the chimney? Rudy looked, but Santa was nowhere to be seen. He must still be arranging the toys around the fireplace in the house below.

The cat was nearing the edge of the roof. Rudy had to act quickly, but he was momentarily frozen where he stood, thinking of all the things he should have done instead of going on and on about the stars. He should have been watching her! What kind of a guardian angel are you, he scolded himself.

A puff of snow brought him to his senses. The fiendish cat had dropped off the roof onto a snow-covered shed next to the farmhouse. Rudy glanced around at the chimney, but Santa still hadn't returned. Rudy couldn't let Sandra disappear out of sight. He hopped off the sleigh and took off after the cat, which was now crossing the roof of the shed below him. The cat heard Rudy and turned to look disdainfully at the mouse scampering after him As he did so, Sandra moved, and Rudy could see that she was still alive.

The cat resumed his descent, dropping over the far edge of the roof onto a pile of split logs stacked against the shed. Rudy jumped off the roof of the house onto the shed, but by the time he got to the edge, the cat had vanished. Rudy looked down at the snow and saw fresh paw prints that turned and went under the shed. The cat must have his den there, thought Rudy.

Screwing up his courage, Rudy flung himself off the shed roof. He was no flying squirrel, however, and crashed headfirst into the frosty white blanket beneath him. Pulling himself out, he plodded through the deep snow to the place where the cat's tracks disappeared. Rudy looked inside and saw the cat staring back at him, Sandra still hanging limply from his mouth. The cat's yellow eyes were two dim lights in the darkness under the shed.

As they stood looking at each other, Rudy heard Santa's booming voice on the roof. "Merry Christmas to all, and to all a good night! On Donner and Blitzen." The sleigh lifted off the roof, flying directly over them as it headed off toward the next farm.

"Santa!" called Rudy as loud as he could, but Santa couldn't hear him. "He must not have noticed we were gone," Rudy moaned. Now what was he supposed to do?

Chapter 5

The cat hadn't moved. He opened his mouth and let Sandra roll onto the ground in front of him. Was he getting ready to attack?

Rudy swallowed hard. "Mr. Cat, sir," he began, trying not to show how frightened he was.

"Axel, to you," the cat growled in a deep baritone voice.

Rudy began again. "Axel, sir." But what more could he say or do? Even if he got the cat to chase him, Sandra looked like she wouldn't be able to get away. And, assuming Rudy could get rid of the cat, where would he and Sandra go, now that Santa had flown away?

What passed for a slight smile crossed Axel's face. He was obviously enjoying this. An otherwise dull night had been made interesting by the arrival of reindeer on his roof and then the capture of this miniature child who lay in front of him. And as if that wasn't enough, a mouse, of all things, had now followed him to his den and wanted to talk to him. How strange!

"Yes?" Axel replied, not a little impatiently, rolling his head slightly to the right.

By now Rudy had determined which way he was going to jump if the cat came at him. "You really shouldn't have done what you did," he said, gesturing toward Sandra. "The little girl you have captured is very important. And when her father finds out what has happened, your life will be very miserable."

Axel's smile broadened. It was obvious that he was so rotten, the more Rudy convinced him he'd done a terrible thing, the more he liked it.

"Tell me more," he said, his eyes getting that sleepy look cats get when someone is petting them.

Rudy frowned. "Besides," he said, taking a different tack, "I hear that people don't taste very good. Particularly skinny little ones like her."

Axel looked directly at him. "How kind of you to be so considerate. I shall find out for myself, however."

Rudy winced. He hadn't wanted to turn the cat's attention toward Sandra as a tasty meal. He forced himself to go on. "She can't taste half as good as a tender mouse from the North Pole, fattened up on the best table scraps a mouse ever ate."

Axel's eyes narrowed. He seemed to be measuring Rudy. "You do seem plump," he agreed, with evident satisfaction.

"Plumper than her," Rudy quickly added.

"Then why not come closer?" Axel asked nonchalantly.

"Because I want you to let her go. Then you can have me," Rudy said.

A puzzled look passed over the cat's face. "You want me to give up what I have caught, fair and square, and, in return, you will take her place?"

Rudy nodded.

Axel was having trouble understanding this. "Why would you do that?" he asked. "Why would a mouse let himself be eaten by a cat in order to save a little girl?"

25

"Because she is my friend," Rudy answered softly and simply.

"Did you promise to do this?" Axel asked.

"Not exactly," Rudy said, wondering whether this is what the angel meant when she asked him to look after Sandra. "She is my friend. And I promised to watch over her."

Suddenly, Sandra stirred, trying to sit up. Axel put a paw on her legs. She saw Rudy crouching at the entrance to the den and cried, "Rudy! Run, Rudy! Get away!"

Rudy didn't move. Sandra pushed Axel's paw down her legs so she could sit up. The cat shifted himself to one side to block her from running away.

"Why don't you run, Rudy?" Sandra begged.

Axel answered for him. "Because he has offered himself in your place," he said, sneering. "And I am considering it."

Sandra looked at Rudy. "Don't, Rudy!" she pleaded. "Can't you see he's trying to figure out a way to get both of us? Get away, Rudy! Get help!"

"No," Rudy protested.

"She's right, you know," Axel said, his voice sounding smooth and sure. "I am going to get both of you, and all of this silly heroism will be for nothing."

"You're wrong," said Rudy defiantly. "Some things just have to be done. That's all there is to it. And I doubt that you, as a cat, have any idea what I am talking about."

Now it was Axel's turn to frown. "Then why don't you simply walk into my parlor?" he asked, gesturing for Rudy to come closer. Axel sounded like he was getting tired of the game they were playing.

"No, Rudy," Sandra cried once more. "Please save yourself."

Ignoring her, Rudy drew himself up. "You let her go, and I promise I won't run," he declared.

Axel answered impatiently, "You wouldn't stay."

"Yes I would," Rudy insisted.

Sandra realized that Rudy would stay, and her heart filled with gratefulness. Something about the cat, however, made her begin to suspect that he might not be as bad as he made himself out to be. "You know something, Mr. Cat," she said, looking straight into his eyes, "I think you're a big bag of wind!"

"Shut up," the cat snarled, pushing down on her leg. "And the name is Axel."

"Okay, Mr. Axel," Sandra continued, "you've already said you're going to eat me. What worse fate could there be than that? Only you're not going to do any such thing, because you're just a big bag of wind," she repeated.

"Sandra!" Rudy exclaimed, starting forward.

"Rubbish," the cat said. "I've had enough of you two."

"Then go ahead," Sandra challenged him. "Go ahead. Kill me!"

She turned her neck so Axel could strike her. The cat held up one of his paws. "With these claws, I could rip your head off," he snarled.

Rudy shuddered and looked away.

"Come on," Sandra continued, her eyes tightly closed, her neck exposed. "Get it over with."

Rudy peeked. Axel stood there, his claws opened, but he didn't move.

"See?" Sandra said, opening her eyes. "You're not a tiger. You're a tabby."

Axel slunk back. "I could cut both of you down with just one sweep of this!" he hissed, slashing his claws in front of Sandra's face, but he didn't touch her.

"No you can't," she said, getting up. Sandra stood next to Axel. Rudy wanted her to run. He wanted to run. "You can't hurt me," Sandra said to the cat, "because you don't want to."

Axel dropped his head. "I used to," he said in a subdued voice. "At least, I think I did." The noise he made sounded like a sniffle.

Rudy suddenly found himself feeling a little sorry for Axel, and Rudy could tell that Sandra felt the same way. She spoke to Axel gently. "So, you were only pretending up there on the roof?"

"Oh, no," Axel protested, picking his head up, "I'm good at catching mice and birds and whatnot. It's just that when I have to bring them home and . . ." His voice trailed off.

"You can't bear to do it," Sandra said, finishing the sentence for him.

He nodded. "Too many saucers of milk, I guess," Axel muttered.

"Then why did you have to act so mean to me?" Sandra asked, a little angry now that she felt confident Axel wasn't going to hurt her. "If you knew you couldn't go through with it, why frighten me and Rudy to death?"

"I don't know," Axel replied. "I guess because it's Christmas."

"Christmas!" Sandra and Rudy exclaimed together.

Axel nodded. "I get like this every Christmas." He made a face, looking like he'd just eaten something that tasted very, very bad.

"Is it because you don't get any presents?" Sandra asked him.

Axel shrugged. He had told them how he felt, but he had no idea why he was so grumpy at Christmastime.

"Or," Sandra continued, thinking hard, "is it because Santa delivers presents to the children, but there's nothing Christmas morning for the baby animals?"

Axel and Rudy looked at her with big eyes. Then they looked at each other. Rudy thought there was something vaguely familiar about what Sandra had just said. He suddenly realized that this was what had been bothering him on the night the little angel delivered Sandra to the North Pole. Rudy had felt left out. Santa's entire household had spent a year making presents for all the children in the world, but none for Rudy's own little ones.

"Why shouldn't the baby animals get presents?" Rudy asked.

"Doesn't a puppy deserve a bone wrapped in a red ribbon? Doesn't a kitten deserve a box of catnip?" He looked toward Axel, who nodded his head in agreement.

"Wow!" Sandra exclaimed, jumping up and down. "What a wonderful idea! We'll make presents for the animals!"

They all smiled at one another for the first time.

"But wait a minute," Sandra said, interrupting their fun. "How will we get back to the North Pole without Santa's sleigh? We're stuck here in Minnesota, with no way to get home."

Their faces fell. What were they going to do?

Just then a shadow flew across the entrance to the shed. Rudy looked up. "It's Santa!" he shouted. The sleigh had returned, gliding in over the trees and landing on the roof. "Come on, Sandra, Santa's come back for us! We've got to get back up on the roof."

Sandra and Rudy started to run out from under the shed, but they stopped when they noticed Axel wasn't following them. Sandra turned and looked back. "Don't you want to come with us, Axel?" she asked.

Axel shook his head. "Oh, I couldn't go to the North Pole."

"Why not?" Sandra said. "It's no colder there than it is in Minnesota. Do you have any family here?"

"No, there's no one here except the old farmer who feeds me." Axel paused. "To tell you the truth, I've always wanted to travel; it's just that the other farms were so far away."

"Then come on!" Sandra exclaimed. She looked at Rudy to see if he agreed, but his face told her that he didn't think this was such a good idea. Rudy could tell, though, that Sandra truly wanted Axel to come back to the North Pole with them, and Rudy didn't want to disappoint his best friend.

"Uh, yeah, why don't you join us, Axel?" Rudy forced himself to say, trying to smile at Sandra.

"Well, if you think it's okay," Axel said.

"Sure it is," Sandra said earnestly. "You have to help us with this new idea. Hurry up or we'll miss the sleigh."

The three of them scampered up the pile of logs against the shed and climbed onto its roof. Axel took Sandra by the neck again, raced across the snow, and leaped onto the roof of the farmhouse where they found Santa walking toward them, following their tracks.

"Sandra!" he exclaimed when he saw his daughter hanging out of Axel's mouth.

"It's all right," she called back. "Axel's our friend."

Axel put Sandra down and stayed where he was.

"What happened?" Santa asked, coming up to them. "I got to the next house and looked back to see why you weren't laughing at my stories, and you were gone! I was so frightened. I couldn't imagine where you were." His concern gave way to a little anger, now that he could see Sandra was safe. "I told you not to get off the sleigh, didn't I? I've got a busy night, and I can't have you jumping off to go exploring every time we set down."

"I won't do it again, Father," Sandra promised, taking his hand. Axel was worried she would tell Santa what he'd done to her, but she didn't say a word. Instead, she introduced him. "Father, this is Axel. He lives here, but he wants to come back with us to live at the North Pole. Can he, please?"

Santa groaned. "You know I don't have enough room in the sleigh with all the toys this year, Sandra."

"Yes, but we've delivered quite a few already, so there's room for Axel now. Say he can come, please?" Sandra smiled up at her kindly old father.

"Oh, all right," Santa agreed, for he could never resist Sandra's sweet smile. "Come on, Axel, hurry up. We've got miles to go before we sleep."

They all piled into the sleigh and took off over the chimney.

Axel sat up, letting the wind whistle past his ears. He had never gone so fast in his life, and he loved every minute of the speed and the wind and the cold.

Chapter 7

Sandra didn't tell Santa about making toys for the baby animals until a few days after they were back at the North Pole. She hadn't wanted to bother him on Christmas Eve, when he was busy delivering presents. When she thought Santa was rested, she went to tell him her wonderful idea.

After their talk, Sandra went out onto the front steps where Rudy and Axel were sitting. "Santa said they can't make enough toys for all the children now," she reported dejectedly, sitting down next to Rudy. "And he asked me who would deliver the extra gifts for the animals." Sandra sighed. "Then he gave me a hug and said he wished he could help me, but he didn't know what to do."

"We can make the toys," Rudy said determinedly. "Can't we, Axel?"

Axel nodded. "We have to. There are simply too many lambs and lion cubs who don't get presents at Christmas. We have a whole year ahead of us. We can make a lot of toys in a year."

"But even if we make enough toys, how will we deliver them?" Sandra asked.

"We'll worry about that later," Rudy replied. "I'm sure that if we make the toys, we'll figure out a way to deliver them."

And so the three friends set up little shops around the great house and barn at the North Pole and got the animals involved in making the toys their little ones wanted. The elves helped at odd times when Santa didn't need them, but he gave strict orders to always work on the toys for children first.

One day when Santa was passing by the barn, he heard everyone inside singing. Peeking through a crack in the door, he was amazed to see Axel standing on top of a ladder, stretching out a banner and singing at the top of his lungs. The elves beneath him were wrapping presents as they sang along.

> "Now Boxter makes the box
>> That Giftster fills with clocks
>> And gifts we made last night
>> That Packster packs so tight."

Axel threw a banner across the box and kept on singing.

> "That Wrapster wraps just right
>> In paper painted bright
>> With brilliant reds and blues
>> By Mixter and his crews."

The elves joined in the chorus.

> "Ohhhh, we make gifts throughout the year
>> For every child who's sweet and dear
>> To fill up Santa's magic sleigh
>> With toys for Christmas Day."

Axel continued on alone in his rich baritone voice.

> "But everyone now knows
>> That children shouldn't be
>> The only ones with gifts
>> B'neath the Christmas Tree."

The elves stretched their necks to sing out their reply.

"So, we are helping Sandra too
By making gifts that are brand-new
For pups and kittens born this year
So they can have some Christmas cheer!"

They were about to go on when Santa threw open the door.

"What kind of nonsense is this?" he called out in exasperation. The elves stopped and turned to look at him. "You're supposed to be working on toys for children," Santa went on, "not for the animals." He looked around. "I bet Sandra's behind this. I told her we didn't have enough time to make toys for the animals, but now I find you all here, singing and doing just that!"

Axel was worried, but the elves were all smiles.

"We're having a great time!" Inkster exclaimed, waving his marking pen in the air. (His job was to make sure the presents were labeled correctly.) "Axel gets us singing, and we simply fly through our work."

"And then," Bowster broke in, waving her arms from inside a pile of bows she was getting ready to put on top of the packages, "we have time to work on presents for the animals."

"Look," Clockster added, his arms usually full of wooden gears, but now filled with a plant Santa didn't recognize. "We made catnip playthings for the kittens."

"And rawhide strips for the puppies," said Topster, whose job it was to make spinning tops that Paintster decorated with stripes. "We can get them *all* made: toys for children *and* the baby animals."

Santa wanted to believe them, but he still worried about not having enough presents for all the boys and girls who deserved them.

"But what if we're not ready on Christmas Eve?" he wanted
to know.

"Don't worry," the elves answered together. "We'll get it done.
As long as Axel keeps us singing, and Mrs. Claus keeps baking us
cookies, we'll have plenty of presents for everyone!"

"Well . . ." Santa mumbled. Then he saw Sandra peeking around
one of the huge posts that held up the barn roof. "This is all your
doing, isn't it, little girl?"

"Yes, Father," she confessed, "but we won't let you down, will
we?" Sandra asked, turning to her friends at their worktables.

"No," they all shouted with one voice.

"But how will you deliver the presents you are making for the

baby animals?" Santa asked. "Even if you can make enough toys, there isn't enough room in my sleigh."

Everyone fell silent.

"I don't know," Sandra answered quietly. The elves didn't have an answer either. Then Sandra perked up, her voice bright and confident once again. "Something will happen, Father. I just know it. We'll figure out a way. We always have so far."

But Rudy, who had been watching from a mouse hole in the wall next to Santa, wasn't so sure. Neither was Axel, despite the hearty songs he sang. He and Rudy had talked about how to deliver the gifts to the animals, but they hadn't come up with any solutions. They always ended up putting it off to another day, but time was running out. They both wanted to believe that Sandra would find a way, but Rudy and Axel grew more and more worried as Christmas Eve crept closer.

Chapter 7

Christmas Eve finally arrived, but no one had come up with a way to deliver the toys to the animals. Sandra asked Santa if he would put them in his sleigh, but she knew what his answer would be before she even asked.

"I don't have the room, Sandra, darling," he reminded her sadly. "I can hardly carry all the toys now. Imagine how unhappy the little girls and boys would be Christmas morning if they woke up and found I hadn't delivered their presents."

Sandra couldn't argue with that. Saddened, she went out to talk to Rudy and Axel.

"What he really meant," she said after a while, "is that I'm too small to make a difference, too little to figure out how we can deliver our toys. Oh, I should never have started this," she moaned, her head in her hands. "Everyone will be so disappointed."

Sandra caught Rudy looking at her. "And don't tell me you're little too," she said, her voice rising a little in anger, "and that we can't all be elephants," which was exactly what Rudy was going to say. "You're not a tiny mouse; you're a regular-size mouse. But I'm not a regular girl; I'm just a tiny child."

Sandra began to cry, but soon she dried her cheeks with a small white handkerchief and sat up. She had a faraway look in her eyes that scared Rudy even more than her anger had.

"What are you going to do?" he asked.

"I don't know," she said. "Maybe there is no way we can get the toys we've made to the baby animals. Maybe I'll give up. I want to make a difference, but it seems that I can't."

Now it was Rudy's turn to scowl. "Well, I'm not giving up," he announced defiantly, although he had no idea what to do. He glanced up at the North Star for inspiration, and remembered the little angel. For reasons he didn't understand, he suddenly thought this was the right time to tell Sandra how she had come to the North Pole.

"Sandra," he began, turning to her, "I was not being honest with you when I told you I didn't know where you came from."

Sandra looked at him in surprise. "You weren't?"

"No. I don't know what your arrival at the North Pole has to do with figuring out how to deliver the presents we've made, but I feel certain it's time that I told you. At least it feels like the right time to tell you." He fidgeted. "Oh, I don't know. I'm not very good at this."

And so Rudy told Sandra about the night she was delivered to the North Pole as a special Christmas present for Santa and Mrs. Claus. As he finished the story, the little angel arrived once more amid a shower of tiny ice crystals.

"Rudy," she scolded him, coming to rest just above the front steps. "I thought you promised me you would never tell anyone how Sandra came to the North Pole."

Rudy didn't know what to say. He hadn't thought about what the little angel might do if he told Sandra the truth about where she had come from.

"Oh, well," the little angel went on before Rudy could answer her, "there are a lot of things I've never fully understood. You weren't supposed to be here in the first place, but you were, and now you're here again. And so am I." This seemed to puzzle her even more. "Anyway, you appear to have done a good job of taking care of the little child," she said, turning to smile at Sandra Claus.

This pleased Rudy, but he immediately began to worry that the little angel would ask him what it was, exactly, that he had done. As far as he could tell, he'd done nothing to help Sandra, except to be her friend.

"What about me?" Sandra asked impatiently. "You brought me to Santa's house, but where did I come from? Do you know?"

The little angel smiled serenely. "Of course I do, my dear. You came from the same place all little babies come from," she said, pointing upward. "From Heaven. But because you were an extra special present, I delivered you myself. Your parents are Mr. and Mrs. Santa Claus."

"Really?" Sandra asked, her face brightening.

"Really," the little angel said. And that was that.

"But can you tell me why I'm so small?" Sandra asked.

The confident look on the angel's face disappeared. "No, dear, I cannot," she said. Sandra's face fell. "But I'm sure," the little angel hurried on, "that there's a purpose here somewhere. There always is. It's just that sometimes I don't know what it is." She sounded confused again.

Meanwhile, Rudy was getting up his courage to ask the little angel for a favor.

"Uh, ma'am," he began, standing as tall as he could, "we were trying to figure out how we could solve a problem we have," he continued, but Sandra interrupted him.

"That's okay, Rudy," she said sadly, "it isn't important now."

"What problem?" asked the little angel.

"We've made lots of Christmas presents for baby animals," Rudy explained, "but Santa says there's no room in his sleigh."

"Christmas presents for the animals?" the angel said, repeating the words. "What a lovely idea!"

"But we have no way to deliver them," Sandra explained.

"Well," the little angel wondered aloud, "if Santa's sleigh is full, maybe you need one of your own." She pointed a long silver finger to one side, and Poof! a little red sleigh appeared. Axel was so surprised he fell backwards off the steps.

Sandra hopped into the front seat. "It's beautiful!" she exclaimed. "But it's so small," she said, looking up at the angel. "Can it carry all the toys?"

"On Christmas Eve?" the little angel asked in mock surprise. "Why, anything is possible on Christmas Eve. The question is, Who will drive it?"

Sandra's eyes got big. "I will," she declared.

"Why not?" the little angel said agreeably. "You made the trip with Santa last year, so you know exactly what to do."

Rudy was standing next to the little angel. He felt like he was interrupting, but he knew one important detail was missing.

"Excuse me," he said, sheepishly, "but who will pull Sandra Claus's sleigh?"

"Yes, who will pull it?" the angel asked aloud. "Santa's reindeer are much too big," she reminded herself, as if going through a list. "And besides, Santa needs each one for his own sleigh." Then her face lit up as if she'd just remembered something. She turned to Rudy. "Have you ever seen a mouse-deer?" she asked him.

Rudy shook his head. "A mouse-deer?" His eyes grew rounder. He looked like he didn't want to hear the angel's answer.

"They're special mice who grow antlers just before Christmas," the little angel explained. She reached over and touched Rudy, a smile on her face.

Rudy reached up and felt his head. He had antlers!

"Oh, you look so cute, Rudy!" Sandra called out to him. "Please pull my sleigh tonight."

Axel burst out laughing. "A mouse with antlers!" he howled, holding his sides and rocking from side to side.

"But I can't fly," Rudy protested.

"Sure you can," Sandra said. Then she turned to the little angel. "Can't he?"

"I don't see why not," the little angel said with a smile. "After all, he grew antlers. Besides, I happen to know that the word *mouse* comes from the Latin word *mus*, which is the root word for muscle. So you see, Rudy, you and your friends will be strong enough to pull the sleigh."

Rudy stood up proudly. "Of course I can," he said emphatically. "I'll do it. I mean, we'll do it. We'll all do it together."

"Hooray!" Sandra shouted. "All we need is more mice. You go round them up, Rudy, and I'll go tell Santa."

Before either of them could make a move, however, Sandra noticed Axel climbing back up onto the steps. "Oh, Axel, I'm sorry. I got so excited I forgot all about you. You must come with us too."

"Oh, don't worry about me," he said, trying to sound as if he didn't care whether he went or not. "I've already spoken to Santa. He says I can ride with him this year, just to keep him company."

"But I want you to come with us," Sandra protested. "After all, if it wasn't for you, we would never have come up with the idea of making toys for the animals."

"Well, that wasn't much," Axel muttered, looking away.

"I've got it!" Rudy said excitedly. "We need a way to let everyone know we've arrived with presents for the baby animals. Santa leaves his presents in front of Christmas trees and fireplaces, but animals don't have chimneys in their homes. We can use Axel's booming baritone voice to announce our arrival at each place we stop."

Axel looked surprised.

"A Christmas crier," the little angel said, nodding her head. "But can he sing?" she asked.

"He's got a beautiful voice," Sandra and Rudy answered together.

Sandra turned to Axel. "Won't you come with us, please?" she asked. "We need a crier."

"Well, if you think I can help," he said shyly.

"Hooray!" Sandra exclaimed, giving him a hug.

"Well," said the little angel, "it looks like everything is working out just fine, as it always does. And now I must be going."

"Oh, thank you," Sandra cried, going over to her.

"Yes, thank you very much," Rudy added.

"Good luck, and Merry Christmas everyone," the little angel called out. As she floated up toward the North Star, she showered them all once again with silver ice crystals.

And so it has come to pass that on every Christmas Eve, two sleighs leave the North Pole. The larger one, filled with gifts for children, is driven by Santa Claus and pulled by reindeer. The smaller one, filled with gifts for baby animals, is driven by Sandra Claus and pulled by mice-deer, with Rudy leading the way. Axel, the Christmas crier, sits next to Sandra, his head held high so the wind can tickle his whiskers.

Sandra, of course, is the happiest one of all. The animals love her for bringing joy to their little homes every Christmas. Now everyone — boys and girls and cats and mice — finds a present waiting for them when they wake on Christmas morning, thanks to a little girl who can fit into a slipper, but whose heart is as big as the North Star.

DOUGLAS CLARK HOLLMANN is an intellectual property attorney who lives in Annapolis, Maryland, where he practices law. He wrote Sandra Claus for his two daughters when they were little girls like Sandra and wanted to do big things.

FREDERICK JAMES SMITH is nationally recognized for his book illustrations, package designs, and unique graphic images. Known for his amazing versatility of style, Jim has illustrated the iconic Marlboro Man for Leo Burnett Advertising, rendered the Pillsbury Dough Boy, served as personal artist for Bing Crosby, and created fine art in the form of elegant, realistic watercolors.

Edited by Linda W. O'Doughda, Annapolis.

Designed by Gerard A. Valerio, Annapolis.

Composed in Centaur by Sherri Ferritto, Typeline, Annapolis.

Printed and bound by Pacifica Communications, South Korea.